# Casting Call

"Follow your heart, follow your dreams!"

Written By C M Williams
Illustrated by Michael Machira Mwangi

This book is dedicated to some of my former students at Penns Grove who revived my childlike faith and ability to dream again - you know who you are.

All the world's a stage pinned by SHAKESPEARE
Get ready to perform! Be brave and have no FEAR.

Auditions start tomorrow for the musical, I CAN in my theatre class.
You must get dressed and choose a career to be a part of the cast.

We will tell a story about The Great Depression
About people who lost hope trying to find a profession.

You only have until tomorrow to decide what you want to do
So, choose something you love that's true to YOU.

Jalissa didn't know what she wanted to become. So, her mother took her to the costume store and boy oh boy DID SHE HAVE FUN!!

Welcome to the Costumes and Garments Shop said, Mr. Coco
Try on whatever you want and go loco! Loco! Loco!
Let your imagination go wiiiiiiillllllld
Have fun and be free my little child.

"So, start looking for something to wear, said her mother.
Let's get focused with no more distractions
Ready! Set! Go! ACTION!"

Jalissa dressed up in different costumes with patterns and silly imprints of balloons hoping to find something soon, soon, soon.

Or I CAN BE an accountant making sure everyone's money is secure, counted and in it's place.

I CAN BE a bilingual secretary talking to people in all kinds of languages from different lands.

Or maybe I CAN BE a Brand Manager that will create strategies for different brands.

I CAN BE a court reporter providing word for word recordings of court hearings using shorthand techniques.

Or I CAN BE a nurse helping children who feel sick and weak.

A dentist

or a doctor
is what
I want to be.

Maybe a dazzling drama therapist using storytelling and roleplay to help clients who have emotional needs.

I CAN be an editorial assistant helping staff with publishing journals and magazines.

Or I can be an environmentalist studying plants and teaching everyone to 'GO GREEN!'

I CAN BE a food scientist studying food products.

Or I CAN BE a fitness guru that teaches people who come in all shapes and sizes.

I CAN BE a geneticist studying the inheritance of traits passed from generation to generation.

Or I CAN BE a government lawyer giving legal advice to members from different nations.

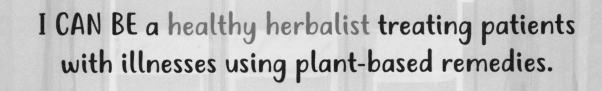

I CAN BE a healthy herbalist treating patients with illnesses using plant-based remedies.

I CAN BE an illustrator creating still drawings for little boys and girls.

Or I CAN BE an immunologist developing new treatments to cure infections around the world.

I CAN I CAN I CAN be a jeweler
creating and selling beautiful jewels.

Or I CAN BE a journalist writing and editing stories that are cool.

I CAN BE a landscape architect
creating beautiful gardens and parks
that look picture - perfect.

So much to choose from, so much to decide. Who will I be? I must look deep down inside! What do I like? What do I hate? I must believe in myself and not be afraid.

So long!

Bye Bye!

Go away fear!

While I work hard and watch my dreams appear.

I not only can, but I will.
Get ready world.
There is no time for
me to stand still.

I'm going to sing it
loud and proud.

I will,

I will,

I will.

I WILL BE a meteorologist using a scientific approach to understand the earth's atmosphere.

Or a makeup artist
doing makeup for
brides and celebrities
both far and near.

I WILL BE a naval architect designing and repairing submarines and ships.

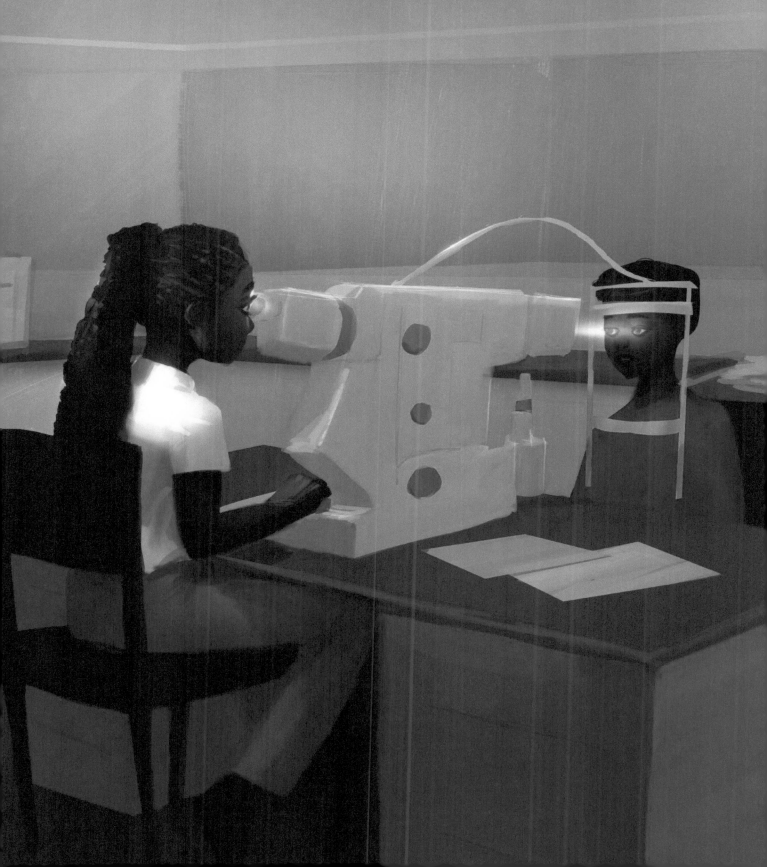

I WILL BE an optometrist treating and diagnosing vision problems for my patients.

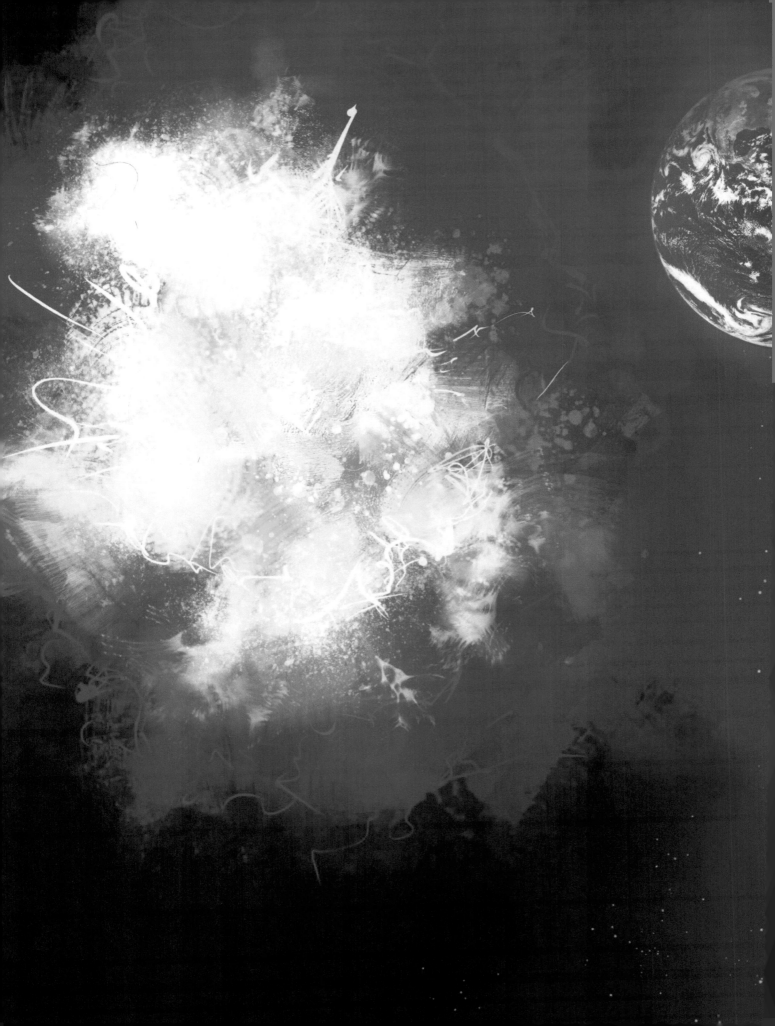

I WILL BE a powerful pioneer like Katherine Johnson whose math helped land a man on the moon. My idea will be so great that it will explode like a starburst in the sky. BOOM! BOOM! BOOM!

I WILL BE a retail buyer who'll purchase stock-from footwear to cosmetics, my styles will ROCK!

I WILL BE a stupendous sports coach

a terrific tour guide

a U.S. representative

or a volunteer worker spreading peace worldwide.

I WILL BE a
wonderful writer

an X-ray developer

a youth leader

or a zookeeper.

I think I know what I will be.
An actress who performs in a play or on T.V.
I can star in so many roles,
making people feel good down in their soul.

I CAN

I WILL

I DID

# DISCUSSION QUESTIONS

**1.** Jalissa went on a journey discovering different careers. What was your favorite career Jalissa explored?

**2.** What three positive words describe you?

**3.** In the middle of the story, Jalissa told fear to go away. Do you become fearful when you try something new? Was there ever a time when you were afraid to try something new?

# CAREER IMPROV

The is a fun improvisation game where children explore careers through role-play and improvisation. This improvisation game will help children to understand their responsibility as an employer, employee, and/or client. Guidelines for improvisation:

**1.** Feel free to use props.
**2.** Use your imagination, creativity, and have fun!
**3.** Create characters with quirky accents and different mannerisms.

———————————

**THE SCENE:** A hairdresser wants to try her new products on a new client.
**Hairdresser's Objective:** You have new products and new hair utensils. You want to use your new products on your client.
**Client's Objective:** You do not want to try anything new. You just want to get your haircut/hairstyle the same way you have been getting it done.

———————————

**THE SCENE:** A police officer has just pulled over a driver for speeding.
**Police Officer's Objective:** The car you have pulled over was doing 65 miles per hour in a 40 mile per hour zone. You want to give the driver a speeding ticket.
**Driver's Objective:** Talk your way out of receiving a ticket. Be creative and make up a good excuse as to why you were speeding.

———————————

For curriculum-based instructions contact: cmwilliams@fayolapublishing.com

CPSIA information can be obtained
at www.ICGtesting.com
Printed in the USA
BVHW020842180121
598043BV00014B/106